HYBRIDS

Nathalia Olymp

CONTENTS

A new Life you say!!!

I woke up after another nightmare. God I really hate those... Looking at the clock seeing it was only 2 at night still. Thinking that I'm glad tonight Charlie has a night shift. God I really hate doing this to him. I just really don't know how to stop. I really want to go back to normal and be his happy daughter again. But how?? I really don't know.

I knew I wouldn't be able to sleep more tonight and decided to get up and clean the house. That is the least I can do. So I did just that. Several hours later I had done the whole house. Even the windows. When I thought that it was several days since I had taken the mail in. Jumping into my shoes and grabbing my jacket I ran outside. God there was a lot in there.I hurried inside, god it was cold outside this morning. It was almost 6:30 and dad would be home in about an hour. I sorted through the mail, getting all the junk in one pile and other posts in the other before sorting trough that one. Dad had gotten 7 letters, mostly bills since that was due in a couple of days. I had gotten 3. Hmm I never get that much, I usually just get the paycheck from Newtons and that's it. Hmm better look at them...

I sat down opening the first one. It had a beautiful script on the front. It was a long letter dated to have been received 2 days ago. Damn I better pull myself together.... It shoulden't have been out there this long. I know dad often forget to get it, so I usually do... Pull yourself together Swan!!!I opened it and read:

Dear Bella. (of course, since it was for me :)) (A/N This (Bla bla bla) means that she is commenting while reading)

I know this letter, will shock you and confuse you, but you must read it all. !! (Well okay, if you say so)Now I can't tell you who I am, but I am here to help you in anyway I can. (Uhmmm Thanks ??)You will receive several papers in the mail, in the upcoming days, that will not only help you, but your father. (Oookay)One more thing before I explain everything I can. You must be better to your father. You and him are meant for something more in this life. You will always have each other. Now let me explain.(That would be great thanks, and I was planning to, you whom I don't know..... Gahhh I'm going crazy here... Bella you can't answer someone that's writing to you in this way... GOD)

I know your heart feels broken right now, but I must tell you it can and will go away real soon. Now you have to believe me, cause what I will tell you in this letter is all true.(That would be nice... Uhm ooookayyy)

Edward is not and will never be your mate!!!! (WHAT!!!!!) He dazzled you and his power still has a hold on you. (WHAT, NO WAY!!!) You must get angry at him/them before it breaks. You see Bella, in the world of vampires, some have what's called temopets. (Called a what now?) Or the whole word temporary pets. (Ohhhh)Example: A vamp finds a human fascinating in one way or another. The vampire will then use its power over them to get them attached to them or even to the coven. The vamp will then use their power to get information. Some use them for sex others just to use up some time in the world. This is what Edward and some of the Cullen's did to you. I know you can find out who if I say only 3 people did not. And too of them you were never close to. (Oh that SOB, how could he. And how could they. GAHHHH I so hate him right now, how can they do this to people... It's the cruelest thing I've ever heard. Make them love you and dump them in a cruel way is FUN to them? Gah...)

Now for the important part: (Like the above info wasn't important... Pfffftthh)I have several things that will change in your life. (Uhmm OOkay)

1: you and your father will change into vampire hybrids in 7 days. In the meantime several things will and must change. (UHMMM A what now)2: you have to tell your father everything. Even give him this letter. (I HAVE TO WHAT!!!!)3: you have to leave Forks. Your destiny lies elsewhere. More info later. (Okay, gladly, but I'm not sure dad would like that.) 4: you both have mates, your dads is a hybrid woman named Cara, and yours is a vampire named Taylor. You will meet them in about a years time. (What, and what now, how the hell do you know?)5: you will both be really powerful and have full control of your powers when you wake up on the 8th day.(NICE)

First I must explain what a hybrid is to you. I am the only one that can make hybrids otherwise they are born. Vamp father/human mother.They can drink blood, but not all do. You both will not need it. You will only eat human food. You will be stronger, see better, be able to fight a vampire or shifters, and you will be able to have children. You will only need about 4 hours of sleep a day.

YOUR POWERS: Invisibility, to change looks, the elements of earth and water, shields (your original mental shield. Yes that's why he couldn't read you. Plus an physical shield) and the power to know. (WOW........)CHARLIE'S POWERS: Physical shield, the power to read and understand people from their behavior and body language, to always know if your safe and well, and to know where you are if your not, and the elements of fire, wind and water.(Way to go dad, awesome)

Lastly but not least: in 3 days you will both get a baby each. This baby is by your dna and yours to name. (We will get what now... aww come on man, I'm only 18)These babies will bring you closer together and will be hybrids to. The only difference in them and you is that your done growing. But they need to. They will grow a bit fast but will stop at the age of 7 when they will look about 17-18 years old. They can't get sick.(That nice to know, but a baby... Really!!!)

In the upcoming days as I said you will receive papers and bank cards/statements. (Uhmmm Bank cards?)You will both have an un-limited amount of money. Well it will be able to last you lifetimes. You will have 350billion each. That should be enough. (WHAT, OH MY GOD) The cards are in this letter, so you can start planing right away. Passports to all countries and papers with names will come in 5 days time. (God this letter must be a hoaks, this is just getting weirder and weirder. But holy cow, I kind of know it's not... WEIRD...)You have 9 houses around the world, papers on them will come tomorrow. (As I said)You will start out in the Canadian home. That is the only thing decided for you.(Only thing decided for us... God like the whole letter wasn't a decision on your part, you unknown person you!!!)

I will write to you later.

Lots of love and healing to you bothFrom Nadia. (Ahh so that's your name.... Nice to know.... GAHHH)

I sat there stupefied for a long time. Just thinking everything over, this was going to be one weird day, I just knew.... I thought to myself that i better just get all the letters over with. And opened the next one. It was a huge folder with a lot of info in it... Apparently most of every info thing had come right away. / Yesterday....

There was, several bank papers, and a lot of stock marked info on what was in our name. (It was even more than what was written in total in the other letter... God she must be crazy!!) There was papers on all the houses, where they were to what was in them, to what they were worth. (A lot of info) There was info on to new cars that was waiting for us at the new house. And papers on the babies we would get... Somehow things had changed from the letter to this paper. Cause, dad would get a boy. (He would be happy about that.) But I would get twins... A boy and a girl. There was even a photo of them in the folder... This was really just to much information in here... But it also made me think. What about school, I was almost done, but what about it, and even my job... I would have to quit, if we were about to leave. This was going to take time to get used to. I laid the folder on the table and opened up the last letter. It was just my last paycheck from Newtons, so no more info there.. Thank god...

By the time I was done it was just over 7am, so I thought as a gift to dad I would make him a good breakfast, and since I felt a whole lot better after the fight I had in my head about Duchewad it made my day/life so much better.... I guess that she was right about getting angry, and boy did I....

Just as dad came home, the food was on the table. I had made pancakes and waffles and had some fruit cut to put on. It looked really good. I would tell him everything after we had eaten... I just hope that I can tell him everything....

SPILLING THE BEANS...

B ella's pov.

This was going to be harder than I thought. The whole time trough breakfast, my feet were jumping on the ground, I could feel my heart hammering away. I almost thought that dad could hear it.

We got done and dad looked at me. "You look a lot better Bells, how are you" He looked at me with a sad smile. I smiled back. "I'm doing a lot better dad" He grinned... I hadn't called him dad in a long time... I really should start doing that... I've missed a lot of time with him and I kind of really missed my dad... "It was hard but, I'm over him. He never should have gotten such a hold on me.... But I promise dad, that I'm a whole lot better... I'ts just that I have to talk to you dad, its really important and you have to promise me not to interrupt before I'm done, otherwise I wont be able to finish. Can you do that dad?"

I breathed out... He looked shocked... Yea I hadn't talked that much in quite some time...

"Your not pregnant are you" He looked like he was about to blow...

"NO dad I'm not, I haven't even..... Uhmmmm, you know" I waived my hands around... I was as red as a sea of blood, but he started to be the same and made a sign for me to keep going and sipped his mouth, grinning...

"You see dad, since I came here to live with you a lot of things has changed. I thought the world was normal, but I found out it's not" He looked like he was about to say something but I stopped him...

"I will explain dad, please no interruption..." He nodded and I co ntinued... "Anyway..... I found out a lot of things in a really short time..." It took several hours but I finally told him everything... Even the tiniest bit of info that was useful in anyway. We talked for hours and hours, and I showed him the letter and folder. He was frozen for quite some time.. Just like I was earlier. "A son, 350 Billion... I don't understand.."

"Me either dad, but I already know its true. I think it has already begun dad." I looked at him with a pleading look. Somehow I just needed my dad. He opened his arms for me and I almost jumped into them. We sat like that, him hugging me tightly to him for a really long time, we even ended up falling asleep, I understood that he did, he had been up for an extremely long time. I guess it was about 5pm we fell asleep. I woke up again, still in his arms at 2. Felling stiff and sore from being in the same position for so long. I tried to get up without waking him, but I ended up doing just that... He held me tighter for a tiny bit. "I love you Bells, you know that right?" he whispered to me...

"Yea I know dad, I love you to." He let go and we both stretched our muscles. popping a few.

"Hungry?" I asked him, and his stomach answered, making him grin and nod... I jumped up to make something to eat. After a bit he came out to the kitchen...

"Well Bells, I've been thinking, if all this is true and our life's are about to change, we better start getting ready ourself's, I don't want to stand somewhere I know nothing about, and we both know we will have to quit our jobs. And I guess you can talk to your school. I know you had all AP classes in Phoenix and really just needed a bit here, so I think you would be able to graduate before we leave if were lucky. I will talk to them at work, I will use my vacation time while my 2weeks notice is used. Using some excuse to get it all done. I will buy a bunch of boxes and we can pack over the next few days. If I understand correctly we have a bit of time before we have to leave. The change will be done tomorrow, according to the letter you got, so how about we start on the hard work after that?" He grinned... WOW he had never talked that much.

"Yea sounds good dad. And since I have both school and work today, I can talk to the principal, and give my notice up to. Though I will just have to say it's because were moving. But what can I say is the reason. We should have our stories straight..."

"Hmm yea your right... Let me think here.... Hmmm" I just sat there waiting for him. I actually really enjoyed sitting here with him, talking to him and planning our life... It felt like I was really home....

"I got it!" I jumped. DAMN! "I could say that I was offered a job, and we wanted to leave to find a place to live and get situated before starting, and that we could just really use a change in life. I know we really need one, especially if all this is about to change. What do you say kiddo?"

"Sounds good to me. we can even use my prier depression as a means of escape, and you accepting the job. They will likely believe that you would leave with me, for me. Instead of just another job."

"Yea your right, I just didn't feel right using that situation without you mentioning it yourself. I know how hard it is to lose someone you love, even though that love was never given. I am really sorry that you had to go trough all that Bells. I wish I had known so I could have been there for you. I lost so much time with you, cause Renee wouldn't let you come over more. And then you came and HE took my time with you. I just really hope that all this will bring us closer like the letter said, and not make us fall apart, I can't loose you again Bells" He had tears in his eyes, making me jump over to him, hugging him again.

"Me neither dad. Were in this together, forever.... I love you dad"

"I love you to Bells..." We hugged for a bit, before he got up to shower, he had to meet at work at 5. After he left I took my shower and turned on the monster of a computer. That was one of the first things I was going to buy. A new laptop...... It was almost ready as I had gotten dressed for the day. I went trough my files and printed out every result I had from my old school, even the extras I had done. So I would have prof in case they couldn't find it.. Somehow I knew I would need these. It took a long time and by the time I was done it was almost 7. So I got ready to leave. Making my lunch and getting out to the car was the only thing I needed. I was at the school by 7:25, and went straight to the office....

------ I was right, I did need the papers, they couldn't find all of the info on me. Miss Cope ended up getting the principal and we talked for a bit. He said I could take my exam's on Friday. So that would mean in too days. And that would be the day the last letter with Passes and all that would come. The babies would come just as we would be settled in the new house... So that was a good thing. And all we would need would be there, according to the folder papers....

The day went by super fast, some happy that I would be leaving (Lauren) Others really sad. (Angela and Mike...) I went to work after school, and told Miss Newton, that we were leaving, she looked shocked but told me I didn't need to come in for those too weeks. That it was okay. But they needed me today... I got home just before 5, and started dinner. I was making a stew, with most of what we had, so it could be used. Just before 6, dad came home.

"Hey kiddo, how did it go today?"

"Hi dad, it went great. I can take the exam's on Friday, and I worked my last day today. Since it was because we were moving she just told me she needed me today, and she would work out the rest. And I don't even have to go to school tomorrow. I just went today, so I could say goodbye to my friends. So I have the whole day tomorrow to pack and what not.." I grinned.

"That's great Bells... I got everything sorted to. I just have to work tomorrow and Marks will take over from me... He deserves it, so I promoted him. And it will just be paperwork tomorrow so that's good. So we can go get the boxes after we eat, I think with all of our stuff it will be easier if we take your truck. So we don't have to go several times" He grinned. I actually think he is looking forward to all this... I smiled back, and we started eating.

--------- Friday afternoon ------

Done, Done, Done, Done, Done..... YAY.......I know I aced all my exam's... Life had simply just gotten so much easier. I just knew stuff now...

Oh yea our changes had just gone smoothly. It went of without a hitch. I woke up Thursday morning at 6, a new me... Of course it was a bit baffling to have so much room in my brain, and to just have all this info inside it, with what I could do, and all that. I even knew that the Cullen's had split up because of me... HA!! And that Alice had used Jasper and he had found out, that they weren't really mates. He had left with Emmett and Rose. It was so so weird knowing that. And dad looked younger, maybe 3 years or so. He looked like he was really happy. Though he had to work he had a pep in his step that day. It made me smile...

Anyway I was done with school, I was happy, healthy and looked to be almost 20. How cool was that... We were done packing and were leaving tomorrow.

Life was changing but I really couldn't wait.......

New Home and Babies.

ella's pov.

We had just gotten to our new home. (---> Picture of the house.) There was a lot of snow at this time of year, but hey it didn't bother me anymore... And that was just awesome. I was a lot warmer and even had a nice glow. I still had my eye colour though it seemed to shine a lot more.

Our house was just gorgeous. So open and inviting. It was quite huge though, but for 5 people later 7, well it had a great size. I had a huge room just next to what would be my twins bedroom on the 3th floor . Dad's bedroom was on the second, my soon to be baby brother's room was too rooms next to dads. There was a huge bathroom in between. Otherwise it was an open space where we had a library and seating area. On my floor, there was our rooms and a huge bath, an office and a playroom. On the first floor there was an office, living room, a huge kitchen with everything, a bath, and entrance and a place to take all of the wet clothes of, just next to the back entrance and laundry room. And everything was in cool and soothing colors. Dad and I really didn't understand why we had to get so much money if all of the houses and all that was furnished and all ready to go. Of course we had to buy food, but come on..... Well no point in thinking about all that. It was a done deal anyway.

We had been in our house for 3 days now, and had just gotten settled, after looking around our property.Dad and I had just eaten our lunch when there was a knock on the door. Dad got up to get it. I heard him gasp and ran to the door, to see no one there. I looked at dad to see him looking down in wonder, so I looked down to. There on our porch was too baskets, one a bit bigger than the other. I gasped and went to pick them up. A startled cry came from the smaller basket, I handed it to dad, because of this stupid knowing thing, telling me it was my baby brother and he would be demanding attention in just about 40 seconds. I grinned at him and went into the living room again.I sat down on the sofa setting the basket on the table I pulled the blanket off, to find two small little babies laying there sleeping. I thought they were cute, they had brown hair and brown eyes looking almost exactly like I did when I was a baby, just as I looked at them I got this intense feeling of being a mother, I wanted to hold them and keep them tightly and closely to me.

I looked at my dad seeing him with my little brother, it looked so cute, I had never seen him with such a tender look in his eyes. It was like he finally felt whole. I could see the love in his eyes, it was the same way he looked at me. I knew that everything would be okay. That we would be okay. Especially after we went grocery shopping yesterday. We had so much fun, that I felt like our bond had tightened and strengthened, it made me feel safe and truly loved. It was so good to finally feel like the kid instead of the parent. Dad had finally stepped up, and was truly everything I needed at the moment.

I was brought out of my memories by a small cry. I looked back into the basket so see my new baby girl looking up in wonder, but it was my little boy that wanted attention at the moment. I took him into my arms and he settled down right away. He just wanted closeness to me. I knew the girl was about to get hungry. So while I went to make there bottles I thought about what I would name them. I had been thinking about it for a while actually. I had decided on Honor Marie for my girl. Cause she was an honor to get and I felt I needed to give her some of my name to carry on. My boy would get the name Wyatt Beau. = handsome little warrior.

Dad had picked Noah Max = greatest comfort. It was a great name. They could look like triplets if you didn't know. But we did. But I couldn't wait to get to know them.

We would have a long journey ahead of us. But I couldn't wait to take it with them and dad.

Getting to know them.

P ic. The kids. The top ones is Wyatt, on the left and Honor on the right. And Noah in the chair.

Bella's pov.

I was sitting in our living room, just enjoying the babies. It had been just about a month since they came here to us, and my god they have grown. They still look quite young, but their mentality is older and wiser. Wyatt can already sit on his own and say mo-mo and ga-da (Mom and granddad) He was just so smart. I grinned hugely every time he tried to say mom.Honour was more active in a way, she was already crawling away, trying to look at everything. She was my little explorer. Since I got her she was always looking around. Sometimes I think that she might have some form of gift, and my knower thingy is telling me that she can sense danger, and is on the lookout so if there if ever anything that she senses she can warn me, since she can also send warning pictures or red flags as dad calls them if there is ever anything to take notice of. But I really want them to just be kids and have fun, so I don't hope that her or even Wyatt's gifts will have to be used. Wyatt is a shifter - not the bad kind but if anything happens he can change into anything, even a lamp if no one is to know he is there.... It doesn't work on me or dad, since we can sense his aura and since I'm him mom, he can't hide from me, but he still tries to be several things, he loves to be a small kitty and lay in my lap or wrapped around his sister, it's just so cute. He can also get invincible and levitate. Quite cool, but not for a mom who gets heart failure every time she sees her son up in the air.... Let me just say that, that is horrifying till you learn he wont just drop down, no he sores down to his blanket and make the blanket cuddle him. It's quite weird, but we have sort of gotten used to it in this house...

Noah is a jumper, and a strategic. One day, about to weeks ago, dad and I were quietly talking about patrol area's around our house, when a map came out of no were in the middle of the living room, like it was on a gigantic screen. And it looked like we could zoom in and out of the whole city. And several dots of different colours were on display.

Blueish were humans wandering around.Yellow were animals and green were shifters (Like Jake, and yes there were other kinds out there.) And red were vamps, if there was a black circle around them, they were bad, golden if they were good people and a big x over them if they were the Cullen's. It was all lined and explained in the right corner. Even several ways to move them and all that stuff. This was the way we found out that 15km away from us, a small pack of shifters lived in a small tribe there. But they were far enough away that they would never know we were here, unless we bumped into each other in the city when shopping, and dad and I were quite human, so we didn't think they would ever know what we were anyway...

--- 8 months after they changed, ---

Yesterday was a real hoot, we had packed the kids up in warm clothes and taken them out to play in the snow. They looked so cute. They looked to be about 3 now.We spent hours playing with them, dad made snowmen and a girl, because according to Honor there HAD TO BE A GIRL, so that is what he made.. He was just such a softy to them, it was heart warming. I was truly happy that this had happened to our family, dad and I had never been closer and we had so much fun together. We even had a mini snowball fight while the kids were making angels. It wasn't until Noah's stomach made itself known that we remembered we had to eat. So we had hustled them in and the rest of the day was spent watching movie after movie and cuddling on the couch.

I can't believe how the time had just flown away and our lives had changed so much. Since we moved here I had spent a lot of my time in my homemade office that was on my floor of the house. I had started writing and had many books already finished and waiting for me to get the courage to send them out, but otherwise I had several stories out on my own homepage: Fanthommomwrither.org (made up, sorry if it is out there in anyway :)) There was many fans to my page and i felt like I had friends, but I didn't need to be with them, just write and be there. Some were even a draft of my books, and I had written it in, to say that there was a book written in a larger scale that I was trying to get out. Just to get some feedback. I love spending time in there and as the kids grow older, they have more time playing than being right next to me all the time. Plus they needed more sleep than I, so that was great in that way. Dad even found his fun writing and we sometimes sat in the same room just typing away. Dad was writing crime and mystery novels, and handbooks to officers. He had several out there already and had almost talked me into publishing my work. I guess I'm just still really shy about this, but I have thought about it... It could be a great way to spend eternity, making people smile with what you write,or even help people in some way or another...

I even started online College in English and writing, and some cook-ing classes to learn several types of food, so we don't always eat the same.

Life was more exiting now, but my mind kept going back to our mates that was out there. I had recieved a letter, with some small info on them to weeks ago and it kept going on and on in my head.

Your dads is a hybrid woman named Cara, and yours is a vampire named Taylor.From the letter I got in Forks.

The new letter:

Dear Bella.

A lot has happened in your life these last couple of months and I know that you must be on a bit of an overload, but sadly I bring more to you. But I think this is something you will be happy about... :) You see I wanted to give you and your dad some info on your mates. Not a lot, since they should tell you about themselves, but I wanted especially you to be prepared on what is going on. You see Bella, your mate is no normal vampire out there, you see he is known to be fierce and cruel to those whom deserve it. He can be a hard man and is often called dominant. He is much like the Major, you know him as Jasper. He had a tough upbringing but he unlike Jasper, didn't run away, he handled his sire and made everything safe from where he was. He has no scars and is known to be able to kill with a look. But don't worry Bella, he only does it to those evil at heart. He can cense these things, that is one of the reasons you are his mate, you are the most pure hearted person out there and he will be able to help your kids with their powers.

With Cara, things have a different approach, you see your father will get a wonderful woman, but she has been trough a lot in her life, and she can remember it all. For him to understand her better with out knowing the details, I found it best he knew before hand so he didn't just jump her without her starting things in the beginning. You see Charlie, your mate had a really hard life. She was born in 1760 and as it sadly often happens, with a normal human mother and a hybrid baby, she killed her mother to be born, this has made her (and a lot of other hybrids sad and scared in life, and make them feel like killers and bad people) This is the same with Cara. She is often scared and lonely. Though luckily she has a much smaller version of Bella's gift of knowledge, and had done quite well for herself throughout the years, though it has never been a piece of cake, for a lone female, so she is quite werry of other people. I think you will handle things well Charlie. I will let them tell you all about themselves and hope you'll all have a happy life.

This is what I will leave you with. Use it for good and make sure you don't judge. Love ain't as blind as many say... So they will know if you get scared of them and how they act in sertant times...

Love Nadia.

So you can see why my head, but of course dad's to, is swirling with info and several plans on how to react in sertan situations. But it wont matter until it happens anyway. We will just have to hope that nothing bad will happen.

I was shaken out of my thoughts as Honor came running into my office. "Momma momma come help me. Noah is stuck in his room, the door won't open." she yelled as she ran back out. My, I still get shocked that they talk so nicely even before they were a year old... Anyway I ran downstairs to see Wyatt trying to push at the door. He looked sad when he saw me coming.

"I'm not strong enough momma" He almost cried. I hugged him tightly to me, and smiled. He's my tough little man. He sometimes acts like he have to protect me from everything. He's going to be a great mate to someone someday. I stood up again and pushed a little harder to the door and it opened up, to a crying Noah whom jumped into my arms. (I sadly think that he forgot, he could use his gift of Jumping from room to room, but that is or shy and quiet Noah in a pot. I'm just happy that he remembers if there is a danger to them.)Dad came in hearing his son cry. It looked like he had been running. He must have sensed his distress. He rushed over to us and took Noah out of my arms, looking at me with love in his eyes.

"What happened Bells?" He said as he padded all around Noah to check for injuries.

"He got the door to his room stuck so Honor came to get me. I just opened the door when you got in dad. It's nothing major, I just think he got scared of not coming out again to us dad. You know how he is. Not liking it if he can't see us or hear us. And he couldn't hear you." I said.. He nodded and carried Noah down to the living room. Boy what a day. I took my kids hand and we went down to... It was movie time before bedtime...

All chaos was gone for now....

Meeting my mate.

P ic of Taylor, as I imagine him...

Taylor's pov. (yay)

I have been wandering this earth for a really really long time, since about 1623 there and about, and sometimes I just wish that someone would be strong enough to take me out. The Volturi was to afraid to, even with the twins in their clutches. They were even to afraid of me to use their powers on me. I'm not that bad, I just take care of what I love. I had been fighting in the English civil war in the first round (1642–46) (The war ended with the Parliamentarian victory at the Battle of Worcester on 3 September 1651.) I was 19 when I joined (Not freely) and got away as I was changed in 1645, at 22 years old.------->>>>I traveled into the woods and lived there for Years and years until I dared to come out. Sadly I shouldn't have done that, I didn't know of my powers so I had to go with my captures. And dragged into another war... The south.... Not fun I should tell you, but I quickly learned a few things about myself and how to use it. I was there for 4 years, and managed to clean everything up, I even discovered that my sire was there and had been waiting for me to come out of hiding, even forced me to live of of humans... Yuck.... I quickly went back to feeding on animals. Somehow human blood smelled awful to me. It smelt rotten and unclean.

Its just sad to know that the south I cleared started up again and just ended when I went back there 2 years ago. I (sole little old me) handled it all alone. No one dared to cross me. Some even jumped into the fire by themselves now that's hardcore.... But I let many people go, since they would be able to handle themselves and had pure hearts. But a lot had to go.... Now I just hope it stays gone down there..... To many people die because of those wars...

Life has been hard... But it has been harder for me these last almost 19 years, I believe has gone. I have felt like I needed to go somewhere for a while now, but have shaken it off for a long time now. It got a lot worse about 1½ years ago, just about. I got this huge pain in my chest and it lasted for about 7 months give or take. I was never good with time. But as of late I have felt an even greater need to go somewhere, so I have been following this pull inside me these last 4 months, it started before then, but I had some trouble I knew I needed to take care of first, I had ran across a red headed bit*h and knew I need to end her. She was gifted so it took a while before I got her down. Stupid cow..... I had to plan to do something else and then in the last second something else to be able to get her. Damn. But I got her and she was so stupid as to thank me just before her head burned. She was weird. Anyway, I was following this pull, till I could feel I was quite close to a huge house. I could hear several heartbeats and one that sounded so beautiful that I fell to my knees. I felt like it was calling me home. I had never felt like this before and I almost started to cry. This must be where my mate was. But I didn't understand, was my mate a human?? No their heartbeats were to fast. What on earth were they???

Bella's pov.

Today as I woke up, I knew today was the day. Today I would meet my mate.

My heart fluttered at the thought. I can't believe this is it. I jumped out of bed, it was just about 5am and jumped happily into the shower. Washing and shaving everywhere. I wanted to smell good and be clean when I met him. I fumbled around after some clothes and took some blue and black jeans on with a red tunic and a white vest on. Braided my long hair and went down to get something to eat. Dad was sitting at the dining room table writing away, looked up at me as I came in and did a double take.

"Wow Bells. Why so pretty today?" He grinned at me...

"Well you see daddy dearest, you daughter had this knowing feeling when she woke up, to be told that today she would meet her mate, so she got ready for when he wants to show up. She also knows that your dear Cara will be here in two months and 4 days, just the time is missing" I grinned back, to see him trying not to jump up and down in joy. I knew he wanted to meet her soon and hold her and take care of her, but in a twist of fate, I would meet my man first...

To hours later the kids came down, ate and then started to play in the living room. I loved to watch them play. And I sat there for a few hours when I felt that he was here. Just a little way out in the woods. I jumped up, winked to my dad and grabbed my coat, even though I didn't get cold anymore I still like to huddle up in warmth.

I walked half way to him and sensed that he was a bit scared of what I was, since he knew I wasn't human... So I sat down in the snow, and slowly started talking in a soothing voice.

"Hi Taylor. I know you don't know me and is even more frightened that I know your name, but please don't be afraid of me... I'm Isabella BTW, but I go by Bella. I live here with my father. There is a lot to our story but we would be happy to explain it all if you want to know." I said. I heard him walking slowly towards me, sniffing the air. I knew that he liked my smell and was still confused as to what I am. But I wanted him to ask me. I wanted to hear his voice...

"Hello Beautiful" And what beautiful voice it was. I turned towards him and looked him in the eyes. He gasped and fell to his knees. At first I was afraid but then I thought that if he could feel your soul, and he would be able to see the purity of mine. He must be shocked or something.

"Hi" I whispered out in a rasp. God he's gorgeous.

He slowly moved towards me, still on his knees, and whispered. "It can't be, such a purity can't be meant for me" I was glad that I had gotten all the enchanced abilities or I wouldn't have heard him. I took his hand in mine and kissed it.

"I'm glad you came, I've been waiting for you" I said as soothing as I could. The poor dear was afraid I would disappear...

"You were expecting me?" He said shocked.

"Yes, I've been waiting a while my mate, and I know you want to know about me, so lets sit comfortably and I will tell you everything" I smiled at him. Gosh he was cute. He sat down and leaned up against a tree, and being fast he took me onto his lap before I could blink. I grinned at him and pecked his cheek, before beginning on our tale of our weird life.

It took me hours, but I managed to get it all out to him, and he was expressing himself trough out the whole thing. When I talked about the Cullen's he was livid that someone could treat others like that. He knew some vampires loved the fact that they could play with humans but he simply couldn't understand the allure to do so. He knew how it felt to be used and didn't want anyone else to feel that... But when I told him of my relationship with my father, he looked wistful and I knew that he wished he had a dad to cling to when he felt like the kid he once was. And I also knew that as soon as dad caught on to that, he would be next to him, and be there for him, like he truly was his father. It would be just what he needed. Yes my mate was a tough son of a bitch and could kill anyone, but he still had a heart, and had lost his human life to soon and in a horrific way. When I told him of my children and my ability to get more on my own, he practically glowed and his smile was huge. I snuggled into him at the news that he was happy about that.

5 hours after meeting my mate I took his hand and we walked home.

I heard giggling and a hard but loving laugh of my family and Taylor froze for a second. I opened the door and saw dad stand up. He came over and stood in front of my mate and looked him in the eyes. I felt him shudder and squeezed his hand.

"Hello son. Welcome to the family. We've been waiting for you" He said as he went to hug him. Taylor froze again for a second and then broke down. Dad looked shocked but with understanding in his eyes and sat down on the floor with my mate. I kissed his head and smiled to my dad, then proceeded to go over to the kids. While hoping that they would get to talk a bit.

Wheeww what a day. I thought as I flopped down on the couch. The kids playing on the floor, laughing. Life couldn't be better. I though with a sweet sigh.....

BeLONGING WITH MY MATe...

Taylors pov.

I never really knew that life could be like this. I felt whole and full of peace. My Bella and her family had made me feel so welcome, that I quickly found my place within the family. I even got a sort of father realationship with Charlie. It's sad that I don't really remember my own father, my family even. I only remember small things. Like the smell of our house on Christmas, or my relationship with my father. I remember that I often went with him to work and came home dirty, but I don't remember what he did for a living. But we were close, that is one thing I really remember, and that I was a big brother. But not my siblings. It always made me sad to think about. I had truly missed that form of relationship, I had with my father, where I could be a kid again and not be this type of monster. And here I found that. Somehow I even became a dad myself, it was weird at first, but now I couldn't think of a thing that made me happier, well besides Bella of course. Just within a couple of hours Bella's children started to call me dad... It was truly shocking, but it made me sort of glow from deep inside.I really love this tiny family.

I truly loved spending time with Wyatt and Honor, even Noah had a special place in my heart. They loved playing tag in the garden or go exploring in the woods near the house. They wanted to learn everything and they did it at an alarming rate. We sometimes had to teach them things a teenager would learn in school to get their minds to shut up. When it was learning they felt happy. God I'm glad I'm not growing up so fast, but as I've come to love Bella's kids like my own, I often felt sad that they really didn't get to be kids. Of course they often had periods where their kids side took over, and played in the snow or Honor would play with her dolls. I loved time like this. Even reading to them made me feel like I was truly with my family now. But nothing could compare to laying next to my mate at night. Holding her in my arm till she was ready to face a new day. No one could hold the amount of love I held for her in my heart. When she told me about her life so far and how she became what she is, I had felt this huge need to protect. Not just her but her whole family. Even Charlie meant the world to me. I would do everything to protect my family. And if I ever saw those bastards to Cullen's, they would get just a tiny bit of my powers turned against them. To find out that THE bastard to the major was with them, oh he and I would have a heart to heart if we ever met. I was having some trouble coming to terms with him saving my mate and him being a good guy. But I'd just have to see later on. Cause I could just feel that we would meet them again. But the young kid Edward. Oh he was mine to play with. Oh he would feel the pain he had put my mate trough. No one would get out of my sight with even hurting a hair on her head.

SHES MINE!!!!!!!!!

my new mother.

Bella's pov.

Time had gone by much to fast. I had just gotten my children, then I got my wonderful mate and life just flew by. We had spent so much time getting to know each other and it was all consuming and just wonderful getting to know my man from within, and not just what the letter told me. I knew of his hopes and dreams. Especially the ones he got after hearing of my life and what I had and could give him, but most importantly to him, what he could give me. I fell more and more in love with him as each day went by.I loved how he got along with both dad and the kids. They loved to play with him outside, while dad and I sat together writing or just had some daughter, father time... It took us a few weeks to be intimate, but I think it made us feel closer to each other and grow our bond tighter together.

But what I knew of today would be more special. Dad would be getting his happily ever after today. I couldn't wait. I knew that he would meet her in the meadow he had discovered several months back, it was where he went when he needed time to himself to think. I had told him earlier when I got up, that he should take a day for himself and go there. That I would hold down the fort so long. He just laughed and nodded. I couldn't wait to meet her. But my darn gift told me he wouldn't be home for another 52 hours. I just hope Noah will be okay with that. He was a clingy daddy's boy, but if he knew dad was away to go find his mamma, he would be fine, so that was what I was going to say, when he becomes clingy. He is such a great kid, but damn I didn't know anyone could love dad more than me, but he beet me by several miles, that one......

Charlie's pov.....

I had felt weird these last couple of days. I felt like some part of me was pulling me in another direction and today when Bells said I should take a day to myself, I felt like I really needed it. If I was going to blow in some way, I didn't want to do it in front of my kids and grand babies. So first I just ran around, needing to blow of some steam. I think I ran for hours.

As I stopped I noticed I was in my favorite spot. Here was where I fully came to terms with my life, that there was friends that I lost because of our hastily move, but it was also here that I dreamed about meeting my mate. I had been so lonely since Renee left me and took Bells with her. I never knew how much I loved that kid until she wasn't with me anymore. And I was pissed at Renee for treating MY BELLS like she was a maid and her housekeeper. Finding that part out, made me want to kill her, but I knew she would suffer hearing that she and even I died and she didn't get a penny. But of course that won't happen for another year or so. But Bells wasn't talking to her anyway, so that part was good, now that our life's had changed so much in just over a year. Damn had it really been that long? Man times fly by.

I can't believe I had the chance at being a dad again. And to a cute as a button baby boy. But he wasn't really a baby anymore. I wish that time would slow down so I could enjoy them more. But sadly they were hybrids to and would grow really fast. But the good part was, that I never had to think about him growing old and dying on me.... Even just the thought made me choke up. I couldn't think about loosing my kids, even my grand kids, it hurt to much. It felt just like yesterday that they came to us, and I remember when my boy stated to walk, and talk. It was moments I missed with my Bells, so I always felt tears come when it happened. I remember when he tried to walk, I was in my office and Bells yelled for me to hurry. I almost fell over my own legs, thinking something had happened. But when I came in, I saw my boy looking rather serious and determined, he was looking my way, but hadn't seen me yet. And started to walk towards my office. 5 steps and bam, he was on his butt. He looked like he was about to cry, when he saw me. I was looking at him with pride. He stopped his shivering mouth and a grin made it there. And just like that he started clapping. Man he was just so sweet. My little man. !!

I really hope that my mate will love my family as much as I do, or I would be in big trouble...

I laid down on the grass to think and just relax for a while, knowing Bells would be mad if I came home already. I really can't say how much time went by, when this wonderful enticing smell came near me. I jumped up, wanting to find that alluring sent, but was met with a whimper and saw a gorgeous woman jump back and cover near a tree. Damn.......... Just then my mind went into overdrive, I knew who this beauty was to me now and why she smelled so good. I also remembered Bella's warning about how I should react and my jumping up didn't help the matter.... Dammit...........

I slowly walked towards her, but stopped before I got to close. I didn't want to frighten the poor thing... I felt the need to sit down, so I was smaller. Sometimes my Police mind got into gear in different situations, and I had been in situations like these several times, both with kids and adults. Sadly it happened more often than what people thought. And with me not knowing what has happened in her life, I wasn't sure, how to proceed... I knew I needed to talk slowly and not touch her until she gave permission or till it was absolutely necessary, witch with her being a hybrid would be tough to tell... But she might need me in another way, I really didn't know, and would have to work with the flow, as it came.

So I sat down on the grass, within grasping distance, but still far enough away so she would feel that I meant no harm....I sat there for about an hour, before she began to move her head to look at me, the poor dear smiled a small smile when she saw me looking at her with a smile on my face. God she's gorgeous.

"Hi sweetheart. Please don't be scared. I won't harm you in any way. Are you alright.?." I asked.

coming home.

Cara's pov.

I had been running for such a long time. My life had really never been easy. First I kill my mom by being born, then I grow up in the woods that was by the house I was born in, afraid someone would come and find my mom. When no one had been there for over 5 years I went back to live in the house. Buried mom in the garden and lived on the means she had. It wasn't always easy, and sometimes I found myself praying that someone would come and rescue me! Other times I loved being alone and not be bothered by others. Especially after my first time in town. God, people stare. When they don't know you or if you seem better looking than them. I often find myself wishing that people, didn't care for what they or others look like. It's not looks that matter. Of course it's nice to look at, but in matters of the heart, it really doesn't matter.

I was 17 when I met him! I thought he was the love of my life. I met him one night I was shopping in the town next to where I lived. His name was Phillip Everheart Jones, he was older than me, but I've always been smarter and more advanced then others and he chose me!!! I was so happy.

At first. Though. He was great in the beginning. He brought me flowers and sweet talked me. All girls love that, but one night I caught him with an older lady in town. We had been together for 3 years and I was ready for more. Apparently he had been tired of waiting after so many years. I wanted to leave him, I truly did. The first few months everything was fine after he left. But then weird things started happening. I knew I was different and I could smell better and all that crap, but as it was happening I became a little girl again. Forgetting what my instinct was telling me. He apparently knew people of my world cause things changed just after my 21 birthday. -Though I now looked in my mid twenties, I had looked like this for over 40 years. Though the last 19 I had been trapped and prisoned by a vampire whom also told me of what I am. He was trying to get me pregnant and see if he could make another race all together.One night though I don't know how he never came back. When he wasn't back the day after, I grew bold. I packed everything I could get into to bags. (Which is quite a lot if you pack nicely.) he had money and all things exiting there. He knew I didn't dare touch things that was his. But hell I've not been so bold in years.

I ran and ran and then ran some more. Until I found myself at this gorgeous field. A beautiful man was laying there, but I truly hoped he wouldn't mind sharing. I was scared as hell that he would be like Michael, but I felt this weird tug, to go closer.

Oh god!!! Please don't hurt me. I thought as I took a step closer.......

another way.

Charlie's pov.

I had been alone for so long that physical contact was something I almost couldn't remember. I know that I truly loved Renee, until I found out what she had done to my baby girl. That she could treat her own daughter like that was something that truly bothered me. But it also meant that I found it hard to trust again, and now was the first time in so long that I found myself longing to hold someone close to me again.

So when my beautiful mate and gorgeous woman smiled so shyly and beautifully at me, it made my heart sore.

I couldn't keep the smile of my face as she came closer to me. All I wanted to do was hold her close, to show her that not all love was delivered in an evil way.

"Hi" she said in such a way that I couldn't help but smile.

"Hello beautiful" I couldn't help but answer. Cause that was all she really was. In and out. I could tell!

________ 6 months later. ______

Bella's pov.

We had been in need of a big shopping trip for some time now, and I was going to take the trip. Dad and Cara were away on a week trip, to come back the day after tomorrow, so I wanted things to be in order for when they come home.

Taylor were going to have a play day with the kids, so all was going great so far.

I don't think I have ever loved a man as much as I love him.. HE just gets me in every way. We move together and almost never have to talk for each of us to know what the other needs or wants. Its a great way to be together.

I sometimes think about my first love, or what I had thought then, was love.

I had been thinking that my hate for them, would never change, but I also knew that my life now was 100 times better without them using me. Of course I knew of the 3 that were never in it, but they still left without a word. I didn't hate those 3, but I would never forgive them either.

Taylor knew of my feelings, and of what had happened and agreed with dad, that if we ever met them, we had a united front and would stand tall as the powerful unit we were.

I got myself together, and drove into the city. It had been a couple of months since I was down here last. But now we needed all things from food to clothes. It took some time to get there, but it was a nice day out.

I had finally gotten all the food and all the things we needed. All I was lacking was some new clothes for the kids and buy something for Cara and me.

I had gotten several things for the kids though they now look to be about 7 was still growing so I only got a bit at a time but with 3 kids it still got to be a bit more than you bought normally. I had also found a few normal clothes for Cara and I, but we needed some more up standard clothes to, since we had plans of starting some kind of work together soon. I'm so happy that we get along so well and wanted to get some clothes that would look good but still feel good to.

But I never thought I would almost get a heart attack when I went in to the next store. Cause as soon as I went inside I heard the voices of 3 people I had hoped I wouldn't see for several decades to come.

I had just turned around and was on the way out when I heard a gasp of all of them.

As I made it out the door again and ran to my car I heard a huge cry out of "Bella"s

I hightailed it out of there. I needed to go home and warn the others. And I really needed to call dad home again. We needed a meeting and ASAP!!!!

THE CULLEN'S

B ella's pov.

I had truly hoped that we would never see them again.

But after seeing some of them last week, I had a feeling I would meet them soon. I even had to get the feeling that they wouldn't stop looking for me, and had to plan this with Taylor, for us to be left alone again.

But whatever. They couldn't harm me and as much as I hated them I knew I couldn't harm them. Even though I wish I could do so to some of them.

They didn't matter to me.

Only my family mattered.

But God I wish I didn't have to see or hear from them EVER!!!

Sadly it wouldn't be so. I knew they would be here at the meadow and we planed to stand here - all of us as a unit. - They wouldn't get to us. We had more power than them. They would never be able to control us.

I just hope we would be able to leave here, and never see them again....

After standing here for about 15minutes I heard them coming. I squeezed Taylor's hand when they walked out from the woods. Alice was jumping about just like always, but she looked troubled. Ha! Just messing with her visions she gets all weird on us. But I really didn't care. Carlisle looked to be in shock and I could see his science mind working in overload. Well sorry mr, but you won't be getting any info from me. But best of all Edward looked to be in real pain, and I knew he would be mad when he found out he couldn't hear any of us, but it might take a while with his 17' year old brain.

I smirked at them, and relaxed up against Taylor.

None of the Cullen's would get to me or mine.

SMUG.

A /N Sorry sorry. So much has been going on, I just couldn't keep up with it. Plus I must admit that I simply forgot about this website for a bit. I can't promise you anything beside that I will finish it. I just don't know what to write :(and I don't want to write just anything so it ends up like crap. But I do have this chapter and I hope you like. Any ideas are welcome. Thanx for your patience with me. _______________________________

Bella's pov.

"Bella" Alice choked out after I finished looking at them all.

"Alice" I said back coldly. I wasn't going to try to make friends here. Oh no. They would know what leaving me had done. But they were also getting told what I feel about them. I wouldn't spare them, or there feelings with this.

I loved the pain Edward was feeling, and I couldn't help but feel smug about it. He would know what he had done, but that he hadn't broken me, like I knew he was kind of hoping, so he could have come back and make me do everything he wanted me to do. I just knew that I was a plot for him, to marry and see if he could make hybrids with. He had found one many years ago and wanted one, and with my shield, well.... Lets just say he wanted to use me to be more powerful, Alice was in on this. This I only know because I got a surprising phone call too days ago, by Rose....

*

I had been sitting in my office, when my phone rang. The kids were sleeping and Taylor were training dad and Cara in vamp fighting, in case it became necessary. He had trained me the last couple of days, so I was taking a break.

I picked up the phone... "Hello" I didn't want to give anything away, since we hadn't given our numbers to anyone yet. But I also knew that it wouldn't be hard to find for a vampire that were looking for us.....

"Bella, its Rosalie, please don't hang up... It's important. I have to warn you." She said... I knew it was, and I would listen, but also make sure she knew I would never forgive....

"Go on" I just said. I really didn't want to give much away. I sounded like I didn't give a dam, but would listen...

"I know that I've hurt you and I'm so so so sorry Bella, I will explain if you'll let me, but I have to warn you about Alice and Edward. I was with them at the shop the other day, and believe me it was not because I wanted to, but Peter.... Oh yea, Peter is a vampire friend of Jasper and we have been with them since two days after we left Forks, he knows shit as he says, but he told me I needed to go, that it was really important for someone I cared about to be able to warn and help them all, he said... Anyway I went to the home, in disguise, I should tell you I have gifts that only Emmett and us here knows about, I never trusted the Cullen's, but I somehow knew that I had to stay, that it was ever so important to do so. I can hide things I don't want people to know, and well I hid it behind this bitch facade and self pity so I knew Edward would never dig deeper. Anyway I went there in disguise of having to get the last of our things, but they acted like they were really sorry, and buttered up to me to get info. I stayed there for two days, to gather info myself, but couldn't let them know. I acted like I had missed Esme, and used her for more info telling. She quacks like a duck, if she feels like you love her... And boy did she... She told me that Alice and Edward weren't who I though they were. We knew, the day we left that Alice was never Jasper's mate, that she had used him for her own protection and to feel like she had more power. That her and Edward had been sleeping together for years. But Esme told me that she had found out that they had used girls for decades to see if they could make hybrids to hope they could make them have power. And when they discovered that you had a power, they wanted to make you reliable on them, make sure that you would do as told. They wanted us to leave so they could use the dazzle to make you miss them and be more clingy and dependent on them, when they went back to get you. She told me that they had went back a couple of months ago, but that there was a new family living in your house and that the town only knew you had moved but not where... That they had come home pissed and wrecking several things in the house. That Alice was pissed she couldn't see you and they though you were dead, but couldn't find proof. That they had been acting weird for a while, but she was afraid to do anything, since Carlisle made it clear that she had no power in the house beside being his mate. I know she had done a lot to make sure you were safe in the house and tried to make them stop hurting you, but with a power hungry guy like Carlisle as a mate, there was sadly not a lot she could or can do. I love her, but I can't help her. The only way would be to kill her, and I just can't.... Though I also have a slight suspicion that they aren't really mates, but he has some power over her. I know she was abused when she was human, and I think he's been using that against her. But she never told me, so I'm not sure.....

Anyway, I went shopping with Alice and Edward, cause Alice insisted I go, before I left again... When we saw you, it was like a light went on in them, that they knew you were alive. When you ran out, they started plotting, they talked about you, that you had to be alone, and all since they couldn't see Charlie or anyone with you. That they could use that, but they couldn't figure out why you were shopping cause you never wanted to before, that they had to get you soon so you wouldn't be able to get people to help you.

Bella they want to capture you and lock you away, and use you till you give them what they want...

We will come and help you Bella. You mean so much to Emmett, Jasper and I. We are so so so sorry for what had happened, but we were to afraid you would hate us to go looking for you, until Peter told us it was important to contact you. Please please, Bella. Please believe me"

She went quiet, and I could hear her sobbing over the phone. It was weird to hear, but damn it, I believed her....

Now I just had to think about what I wanted to do with this info, and how to use it towards the Cullen's.....

*

And think I did. But damn I never thought there would be this huge consequences from my decision. But I would get to that later...

Now the Swans and Whittlock's were looking at the 3 of them, Esme apparently not involved.

I was rudely interrupted from my thoughts by Edward.

"Bella, love. I've missed you so much, please come to me." He said, though he could clearly see Taylor holding on to me. God what an idiot. I'm just glad that Cara was at home with the kids, They could never see them....

Oh this would be going faster then I thought. Taylor just looked at them.... Wow, just wow....

OH FOR THE LOVE OF GOD, SHUT HIM UP.

B ella's pov.

God I loved it when my worrier looked deadly. Yum. If it wasn't for the damn Cullen's I would have jumped him. I heard Jasper cough. And couldn't help but grin at him. It had been weird when they came home to us the same night as my talk with Rosalie.

First of, when they came they all had a look of shame, yet excitement on their faces. I had thought for a really long time that they deserved to be sad and unhappy, but now.... I just had this feeling that I wasn't the only one that had been used in the family. aside from what Rosalie had told me of course... There just had to be more to it.. I just needed to find out what...!!

I had asked my family to leave for the day, so I could air the house out. I didn't want them to know whom was with me, yet. I had told them all of what Rosalie had told me and they agreed to trust them. And I had been waiting most of the day for them to come.

Anyway, I invited them in, and sat in the living room.

I had moved all the toys to the office, so they wouldn't see. I wouldn't show them anything until I was sure.

Rose looked around as she came into the room. I knew she thought the house was to big for one person, but I wouldn't tell her anything yet.

"Bella, thank you so much for allowing us to come. I know it took a lot for you to allow us in again... Oh and this is Peter and his mate Charlotte" she said as she pointed to a man that looked a lot like Jasper and a tiny blond girl next to him. Since I didn't know them and knew they were associated with Jasper and such I knew they could fight and were good people. I was just finding it hard to trust them all, even though I knew I could...

"Bella, I just want to say that I'm really sorry about your birthday, though it was their bloodlust that was transferred into me, it was still awful of me to do what I did" Jasper looked down on the floor. I sent him my understanding and trust, and hoped he understood what I just couldn't say. He had always been one of my favorite in the former family. I had always been sad that I was never allowed to get to know him.. He always seemed to be a really nice man. One that always had a good head on his shoulders...

I knew this conversation were going to be tough. I just didn't know what to say to any of them really... What could I say really, they knew they had hurt me. I knew they knew, so how could we go from this, to what i felt needed to happen. I knew we would need them. Not so much as the fighting thing, but more to make a statement to the rest of the Cullen's. They needed to know that they didn't have the power here. I knew we could stop them within seconds if it needed to happen. They could never make me feel like I wasn't worth anything anymore...

I would just have to go with my gut I guess.

Anyway. Back to here and now. I stood looking at the Cullen's and god I was bored. Why in the world did I have to see them again.?? Oh yea, cause I knew they wouldn't leave me alone.

As I looked to Carlisle again, I just knew that Rose had been right. Esme wasn't his mate. Nice. Now I knew it would be over real quick. I knew it would end real soon. They couldn't be allowed to leave here, cause if they couldn't get me, many other girls in the future could be taken, and I would never allow that to happen.

I was just about to start talking when the idiot started up again.

"Bella what the hell are you doing with him, you belong with me, come on get over here right now."Edward said while really looking like an angry kid. He looked like he lost his mind decades ago, well I guess the flue took more out of his brain than they knew. "Bella, I'm getting angry now, if you're not over by my side in 5 seconds, I'll kill every one of you."This just made me laugh so hard, I couldn't control it, I felt like rolling on the ground laughing but I knew that was stupid. I heard a growl and looked up. I saw Alice and Edward charge towards us and Carlisle looking on with glee and excitement, it made my anger boil, that he was truly evil. Hmmm. I wonder!!! Oh this could be fun!!!

I looked at him again with a huge grin, making him stumble back. What the hell was that. Vampires don't just do that. What the actual hell??Oh well. The two idiots were still coming at us and My man just looked at them, and wush the wind came around them and they were ash. Damn that was fast. I didn't even have time to use any of my powers. :(Carlisle stood there in shock when all of our eyes went to him. He started to look livid, "this isn't over isabe" he never had the chance to continue. I was so mad. I had apparently crushed him with my shield. Aww but I wanted to get more info out of him.

I pouted and turned in my loves arms. Damn it.

Well, we at least had some peace again. Now we just had to see about Esme. Beside that, I just wanted to go home.

And home we went. When all was said and done. We had each other. We were family. We just had to find out how to work as one.

EXPANDING OUR FAMILY.

It has been 7 months since our so called fight. And I've been loving life. It was tough the first few months, since our now extended family decided to stay close. So we had to figure out how to do things. And we had to talk about the kids. What was okay and all that. Cause I had a feeling that if I didn't Rose would try to make decisions on some things and that wasn't okay. The kids were ours and they had nothing to do with that. They could be aunts and uncles but anything else was a no go to us. Especially when Esme then came to them at first, did we have some trouble. She was really glad that we had taken them out. Yet sad to loose most of her family as she said. But she tried to take over on how we raised our kids, and after I had repeatedly said that she should stop it, she came up with something new or tried to rule the whole coven and not as an extended family as we saw it, and tried to be a leader. And we all know that Esme was no leader type. So in the end I told her that if she didn't follow our rules that she had to leave, they were our kids and our family. That she would never and I mean never, gonna be a mother or grandmother to them, so she had to stop.

Well let's just say that she became pissed. Jasper and to my surprise Rose stepped in. In the end Esme left for the Denalis and we haven't heard from her since.

Beside that it has been quiet, well as quiet as you can be with several children. Plus we just found out that I'm pregnant. Wow. I mean. We didn't think it would happen this soon but we were all ecstatic.I was about 3 months along but looked about 8. So it wasn't long before we would be able to cuddle our baby.Taylor was so happy and extremely exited about being a dad. Though he had taken mine as his, this was different. Something he never thought would happen.

Some other changes that, at first scared the ever loving crap out of me, was that we found out that our loving Major aka Jasper, found his mate in our daughter Honor Marie. I was pissed at first, but Taylor was more, but we talked a lot, and tried to figure things out. I knew that for now all he felt was really protective of her and her loved ones, so for that I/we would give him a chance. I knew there was a chance for her to have a vampire as a mate, I had also known that there was a chance that, it would be before she was grown, but it still hurt, that we weren't the only loves in her life now. But after some time, it all got better between us all. We learned to work together, and talk more. I've always liked Jasper so I knew we would be able to be a great family. The only thing I was a bit scare of now, was if the Volturi ever found out about us, it wouldn't be good. First, we would have to kill a lot of them, but worse we would then have to rule the vamp world and I really didn't want that. So I truly hoped that they would never discover what kind of power we had in our new and rather large family.

Rose, Emmett, Peter, Charlotte and Jasper bought the house about 5minutes away from us, to be closer to us after they came here and all the things happened. It was good that they were in their own house, and still close, cause I really didn't want them in the house, not that I didn't love them, I just really felt we needed our own...

Our kids now looked like they were about 8years old, and were really energetic, Taylor trained with them, and sometimes Jasper was over to. They had been better at talking and I even felt they were beginning to be really close friends. Sometimes, everyone was here and we would all train and have fun together, those time made training a hell of a lot more fun, especially when Emmett, found out he couldn't beat me, even without powers. He could be such a kid sometimes but I loved him just the way he was...

Our future looked bright and now was the time to start our forever. And with that my water broke...... Ouch......

our forever.

50 years later.

Bella's pov.

I sat on a chair on our porch, looking out at our ever growing family. Taylor and I found out that no matter how long we had been together our family grew. After our first pregnancy where our boy Kody was born, we learned how things went and that he truly was a gift from the gods. He was truly a fantastic mix of the both of us. We never loved our children differently, and always made sure they knew we loved them the same, but he was our first together and that made him special. Beside that, our children grew and had families of their own, it was like we ended up with our own little village of sorts on our land. Jasper and Honor have had 5 kids so far, and had a house to our right, where Peter and the rest was to our Left. Wyatt met a hybrid woman 20 years ago named Jennifer. (She was a sister to several other hybrids that we saved from their father and found a brother of theirs named Nahuel with his aunt. We also found out that another of their sisters one of the youngest Saseline was Noah's mate. So yea again we grew. Both boys shared a home across from us, since they were extremely close, and their girls were really close ass well. Since then we've had 12 children and 34 grandchildren. Jykes, that's a lot. But we love each other a lot.

So far all has been quiet and we have had a lot of family times. Though 10 years ago, I had a feeling that there was something coming and soon. I called the whole family together and we had a meeting. Peter came forth that his knower told him that the Volturi would be here within a week. And that it was all of them that was coming. Even the wife's. So we trained and trained some more. We had a lot of powers here and knew we could handle them all within minutes, still we felt the need to get some of our frustration and anger out.. Why were they coming?? Yes we were a giant lot of people, but we never bothered anyone. So this just pissed me off. I had a feeling that Aro just wanted to see if he could get some of us for our gifts, and to see what he could get out of us, but to just try to come to our land was simply not ok...

The week passed by so quick that just 30minutes before they arrived my gifts flared up, with the knowledge that we had to kill Chelsea and Aro. That a lot of them was there under his and her powers, that if they were gone, many of them would be free to live. So I told the family and that was simply what happened... It was over to fast for anyone to notice and lets just say our family got bigger, though a lot of them went back to Voltera. Marcus, found a second mate in Nahuel's aunt and she left with him to rule Volturi, with Caius and a lot of the guards. Some of us promised to help if the need was ever to great for them to handle, but they had to promise that no one would join out of force. That it had to be a happy place to be, and eaisere to find refuge for people that needed it, and not be afraid that they would be stuck there for whatever reason. Things since then have been really peaceful in our world and our family at peace once again.

Just as i thought that, I felt a kick from our newest baby addition to our family. I smiled down at my belly, wishing that our forever would always be this peaceful and full of family.

Our forever was looking good, and I couldn't be happier......